Now I Am

D0607862

Contents

I Am Six

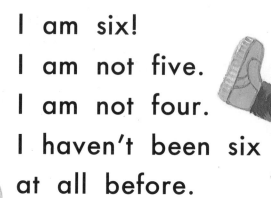

I am six!
I am not five.
I am not four.
I haven't been six
at all before.

Superkid

I'm not
Bill, or Joe, or Sid.
Don't you know,
I'm Superkid?

Loose Tooth

Fred has a hole
Where a tooth used to be,
And so has Jack.
But what about me?

I have a tooth that
is wriggling about.
I poke it with my tongue,
But it won't come out.

I Can Do Anything

I can do anything,
Anything you see.
I can swim the biggest ocean
And climb the tallest tree.

I can tame a crocodile,
Have a dragon for a pet,
Drive a racing car,
And fly a jumbo jet.

I can ride a bucking bronco,
And you'll never see me fall.
I can do anything,
Anything at all.

My Mom Can Do Anything

My mom can do anything,
Anything at all.
Roller skate,
Parachute,
And shoot a basketball.

My mom can do anything,
Anything you like.
Water ski,
Surfboard ride,
And race a motorbike.

My mom can do anything,
Anything you say.
That's why I think
My mom's okay.

Shopping List

I read the list
When we go to the shops.
Flour,
Sugar,
Coco Pops.
But I won't read
O-A-T-M-E-A-L.
I always get stuck,
Because I think oatmeal is yuk!

First Day

Do you remember,
Your very first day
When you came to school?
Did the teacher say,
"Hello, hello, we've someone new.
What's your name?"
And "How do you do?"

Hard and Easy

"It's hard," growled the tiger,
"to climb up a tree."

"It's easy," laughed the monkey,
"and you can't catch me."

"It's easy," said giraffe,
"to reach things when you're tall."

"Well it's hard for me," said the flea,
"I'm too small."

Bigger and Smaller

A dinosaur is bigger
than me.
And so is a whale.
And so is a tree.

But an ant is smaller
than me.
And so is a butterfly.
And so is a bee.

Zoggits

Zoggits live in queer places
And they're very very small,
But they can do anything,
Anything at all.

It's hard to see a Zoggit,
It's hard to catch one, too.
But there's nothing,
No there's nothing,
That a Zoggit cannot do!

You won't find one at the circus,
You won't find one at the zoo,
But if you're really really lucky,
A Zoggit might find you.

Then
   Abracadabraca!
    Whacky dee doo!
There'll be nothing,
  No nothing, that you cannot do.

I'm the Boss

Boss for a day.
What a cheek!
I want to be boss
for a week.

Boss for a week.
Now listen here!
I want to be boss
for a year.

The Letter

Dear Mrs. Macintosh,
I just would like to say,
How are you getting on?
And how are you today?
I hope, really hope,
That you will soon be better.
Now I am at the end
Of my very little letter.
Love from
Tom.

A Book is a Friend

A book is a friend,
A friend that you need.
Open it up
And read
And read.

A Story

A story begins
And a story ends.
What's in the middle?
Well...that depends.

I Wonder

I wonder,
Yes, I wonder,
When I look at all the stars...
I wonder,
Yes, I wonder,
If I could live on Mars?

Sunset

Sometimes I look at the sky
When the sun is going to bed,
And I love the colors I see:
Orange and yellow and red.

Faces

I can make a face that's happy,
I can make a face that's sad,
I can make a face that's scary,
I can make a face that's mad,
I can make a face that's silly,
I can make a face that's glad.

happy sad scary mad silly glad.

The Sea

I went down to the
Beach to play,
And the sea was an
Angry monster today.
It slapped at my feet,
It slapped at my hand,
It slapped at the rocks,
And it slapped at the sand.

I went down to the
Beach to play,
And the sea was a gentle
Lamb today.
It licked at my feet,
It licked at my hand,
It licked at the rocks,
And it licked at the sand.

Please, Mr. Clock

Please, Mr. Clock,
With your tick and your tock,
Tell me the time.

Breakfast time.

Please, Mr. Clock,
With your tick and your tock,
Tell me the time.

School time.

Please, Mr. Clock,
With your tick and your tock,
Tell me the time.

Lunch time.

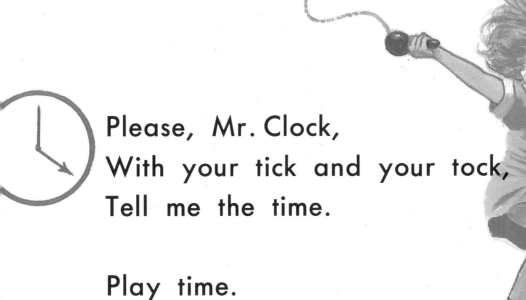

Please, Mr. Clock,
With your tick and your tock,
Tell me the time.

Play time.

Please, Mr. Clock,
With your tick and your tock,
Tell me the time.

Dinner time.

Please, Mr. Clock,
With your tick and your tock,
Tell me the time.

Bed time.

Take a Book

It's raining outside,
I can't go and play.
What will I do
For the rest of the day?

Take down a book
From up on the shelf.
Take down a book
And read it yourself.